THE FULL Alex

Collected Strips
1987–1998

CHARLES PEATTIE
and
RUSSELL TAYLOR

HEADLINE

First published in 1998
by HEADLINE BOOK PUBLISHING

10 9 8 7 6 5 4 3 2 1

These cartoons first appeared in the *London Daily News*, the *Independent*, and the
Daily Telegraph.

Additional material by Mark Warren, to whom many thanks.

ISBN 0 7472 7695 1

Printed and bound in Italy by
Canale & C. S.p.A.

HEADLINE BOOK PUBLISHING
A division of Hodder Headline PLC
338 Euston Road
London NW1 3BH

THE FULL Alex

Charles Peattie was born in 1958 and studied painting at St Martin's School of Art. During the early eighties he worked as a portrait painter, freelance cartoonist and designer of greetings cards. He also produced (with Mark Warren) the legendary 'Dick' cartoon in *Melody Maker*.

Russell Taylor was born in 1960. He studied Russian and Philosophy at Oxford University and, after failing to be recruited by the counter-intelligence services of either Cold War power, drifted into journalism. He met Charles at a Christmas party in 1986. Charles had a commission for a strip for the financial pages of the incipient *London Daily News* and was looking for a co-writer.

The *London Daily News* folded after only five months but Alex was popular enough to be headhunted to another new newspaper, the *Independent*, in September 1987. In January 1992 he treacherously defected to the *Daily Telegraph* where he has appeared ever since. Alex can also be read in newspapers in Australia, Canada, New Zealand, Holland and many other countries.

Charles and Russell (with Mark Warren) are also the creators of the 'Celeb' cartoon in *Private Eye*. Charles is a recovering workaholic who is currently developing comedy scripts for a number of TV projects. He has two daughters and lives in London.

Russell writes film and TV music. Based primarily in the Groucho Club, he occasionally visits his home and cat in north London.

Also by Charles Peattie and Russell Taylor published by Headline

ALEX CALLS THE SHOTS
ALEX PLAYS THE GAME
ALEX KNOWS THE SCORE
ALEX SWEEPS THE BOARD
ALEX FEELS THE PINCH

Alex

Alex's wife Penny.   Their son : Christopher.

Clive + his girlfriend Bridget.

Ruth + Clio.

Rupert
(Alex's boss)

Greg. Alex's brother ; A journalist.

Vince
(a money broker)

1987

THE YEAR OF THE YUPPIE: THE CITY WAS RAKING IT IN WITH STOCK MARKET, PRIVATISATION AND PROPERTY DEALS (AND ONLY THE GUINNESS BOYS GOT CAUGHT), MRS THATCHER'S CONTRACT WAS RENEWED FOR A FURTHER FIVE YEARS... BUT THE GREAT STORM AND BLACK MONDAY BLEW IT ALL AWAY...

1988

PUBS WERE NOW OPEN ALL DAY – HANDY FOR THE LEAVING PARTIES FOLLOWING THE FIRST WAVE OF POST-CRASH SACKINGS. NEWSPAPERS, BULGING WITH ADVERTS FOR LIFE-STYLE-ENHANCING GADGETS, SUDDENLY CARRIED DIRE WARNINGS ABOUT THE DANGERS OF GLOBAL WARMING, AIR TRAVEL AND DEADLY BOILED EGGS.

1989

THE BERLIN WALL WAS KNOCKED DOWN (AS WERE PROPERTY PRICES ALL OVER BRITAIN). NIGEL LAWSON RESIGNED OWING TO "DIFFERENCES IN STRATEGIC DIRECTION" WITH HIS CHIEF EXEC. THE RECESSION LOOMED. ECO-FRIENDLY PRODUCTS AND DESIGNER BABIES BECAME THE NEW STATUS SYMBOLS.

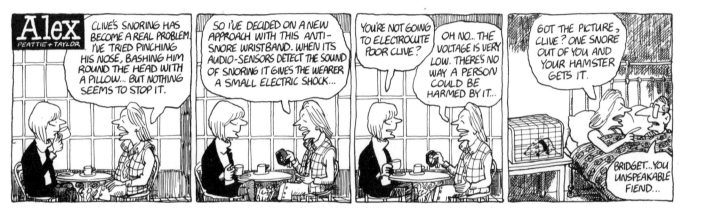

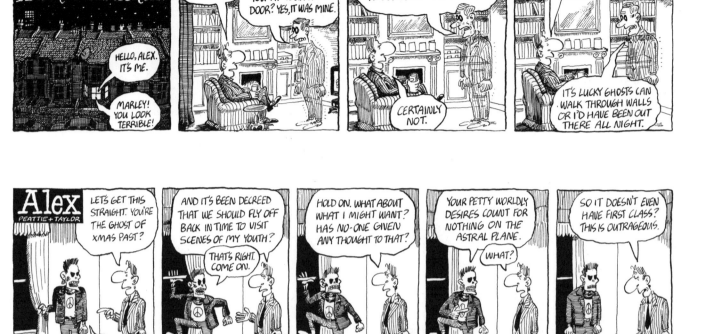

1990

THE "NICE" NINETIES: EAST AND WEST GERMANY MERGED BUT KUWAIT WAS SUBJECTED TO A HOSTILE TAKEOVER BID BY SADDAM HUSSEIN. MRS THATCHER BECAME THE LATEST VICTIM OF CORPORATE DOWNSIZING AND ERNIE SAUNDERS WAS MOVED SIDEWAYS TO HEAD OF TOBACCO TRADING AT FORD OPEN PRISON...

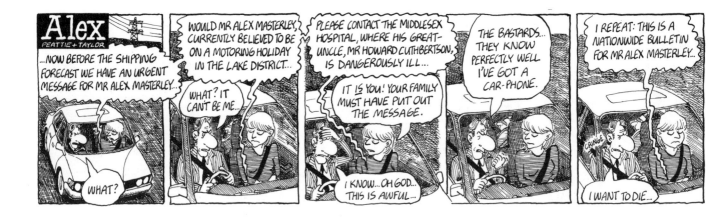

1991

SADDAM'S BID FOR KUWAIT WAS REJECTED BY A HASTILY ASSEMBLED INTERNATIONAL MONOPOLIES AND MERGERS COMMISSION. ROBERT MAXWELL FAILED IN HIS FINAL FLOTATION ATTEMPT AND THE SOVIET UNION WENT INTO LIQUIDATION.

1992

THE CONSERVATIVES UNDER NEW MANAGEMENT WERE REAPPOINTED TO RUN BRITAIN BUT RAPIDLY SUSTAINED LOSSES OF £4 BN UNDER ADVERSE TRADING CONDITIONS IN THE E.R.M.. AN ANNUS HORRIBILIS ENDED WITH THE CORPORATE DE-MERGER OF CHARLES AND DIANA.

Strip 1:

THAT WAS AWFUL. WHEN I HAD JARVIS INTO MY OFFICE I HAD EVERY INTENTION OF SACKING HIM, BUT SOME INSTINCT OR EXPERIENCE TOLD ME I SHOULDN'T.

WHEN YOU SEE A MAN LIKE THAT- TENSE, NERVOUS, ALMOST ON THE EDGE OF HIS SEAT BEFORE YOU BREAK THE NEWS, YOU KNOW YOU OUGHT TO TREAD CAREFULLY.

OH QUITE.

DO YOU KNOW, WHEN I SAID I WAS CONSIDERING GIVING HIM A SECOND CHANCE HE LITERALLY BROKE DOWN AND WEPT.

GOOD HEAVENS.

YES. HE'D ALREADY ACCEPTED A JOB SOMEWHERE ELSE AND WAS HOPING TO GET A REDUNDANCY PAY-OFF INSTEAD OF HANDING IN HIS NOTICE.

GREEDY LITTLE SAUSAGE. I WISH WE HAD MORE LIKE HIM.

Strip 2:

WELL, TONIGHT IT'S A CHOICE BETWEEN JULIAN'S COCKTAIL PARTY AND COLIN'S GO-KARTING TOURNAMENT...

NO CHOICE AS FAR AS I'M CONCERNED, CLIVE...

MAYBE I'M GETTING OLD AND LOSING MY EDGE, BUT I'M NOT REALLY UP TO SPENDING MY WEEKENDS PARTICIP- ATING IN THOSE STRESSFUL HIGHLY- COMPETITIVE EVENTS ANY MORE...

I KNOW WHAT YOU MEAN...

THESE DAYS I PREFER TO RELAX IF I'M IN COMPANY- NOT BE FORCED TO ENGAGE IN PATHETIC ATTEMPTS TO OUTDO ONE ANOTHER IN A FIELD IN WHICH NONE OF US IS MUCH COP.

SO WE'RE AGREED ON WHERE TO GO TONIGHT..

AT LEAST HERE WE DON'T HAVE TO SPEND THE EVENING FRANTICALLY BLUFFING ABOUT HOW MUCH WORK WE'VE GOT ON...

...AND HOW BIG OUR BONUSES ARE GOING TO BE...

Strip 3:

WELL, CLIVE, I'M TAKING 4 WEEKS OFF TO STAND AS THE TORY CANDIDATE IN THE ULTRA-SAFE LABOUR STRONG- HOLD OF GRIMLEY EAST.

WITH THIS DEEP RECESSION IT'LL BE A ROUGH RIDE. I HAVE TO EXPECT ALL MY PRE- ELECTION ASSURANCES AND PROMISES TO BE UNDERMINED BY DIRTY TRICKS AND DISINFORMATION FROM THE OPPOSITION.

AS SOON AS THEY GET WIND OF MY CANDIDACY THEY'RE GOING TO START SAYING DAMAGING THINGS ABOUT MY ELECTION CHANCES.

YES I KNOW...

...ROMBURGS HAVE ALREADY STARTED A RUMOUR THAT YOU MIGHT WIN.

DAMN. QUICK, ISSUE A DENIAL OTHERWISE THEY'LL POACH ALL MY CLIENTS BEFORE I GET BACK.

Strip 4:

RATHER A DEVIOUS PLOY SURELY, ALEX?

NOT AT ALL, CLIVE. ALL BRITISH EX-PATS ARE ENTITLED TO A POSTAL VOTE..

AS A CONSERVATIVE CANDIDATE I'VE JUST ASKED AROUND FOR THE NAMES OF PEOPLE'S FRIENDS AND CONTACTS WHO LIVE AND WORK ABROAD. I'LL BE GETTING IN TOUCH WITH THEM.

WITH THE ELECTION IMMINENT WE CAN'T AFFORD TO NEGLECT SUCH INDIVIDUALS. YOU SEE, THEY TEND TO BE SUCCESSFUL, WELL-PAID PROFESSIONAL PEOPLE AND YOU KNOW WHAT THAT MEANS.

RIGHT.

...SO ANY CHANCE OF SWINGING ME A JOB OUT THERE IN HONG KONG? LOOKS LIKE THIS COUNTRY'S STUFFED...

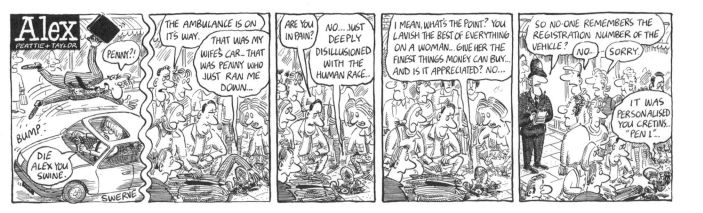

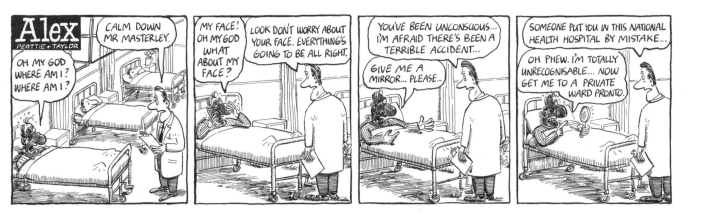

1993

ECONOMIC GREEN SHOOTS WERE RUMOURED IN BRITAIN BUT ASIL NADIR WISELY RELOCATED HIMSELF TO HIS HEAD OFFICE IN CYPRUS. GRUNGE WAS THE STREET FASHION BUT THE CITY STUCK TO RALPH LAUREN ON ITS INCREASINGLY POPULAR DRESS DOWN FRIDAYS.

Alex PEATTIE + TAYLOR

I MUST SAY I FEEL A LOT MORE COMFORTABLE ABOUT SACKING ATKINS THAN I WOULD HAVE DONE TWO YEARS AGO.

THE JOBMARKET OUT THERE HAS REALLY CHANGED SINCE THE BANKS WERE ALL CONTRACTING THEIR OPERATIONS WHEN THE ECONOMIC OUTLOOK WAS BLEAKEST.

AT THE MOMENT WITH THE BUSINESS CLIMATE HEALTHIER, THE STOCKMARKET AT AN ALL-TIME HIGH AND A MOOD OF REAL OPTIMISM ABOUT, IT'LL BE TOTALLY DIFFERENT FOR ATKINS WHEN HE GOES TO SEE HEADHUNTERS...

YES. THEY'RE BOUND TO REALISE THAT HE WAS USELESS AT HIS JOB.

QUITE. WHEREAS IN THE OLD DAYS HE COULD HAVE CLAIMED HE WAS JUST A VICTIM OF THE RECESSION.

Alex PEATTIE + TAYLOR

THIS PHOTOGRAPH TAKEN BY ONE OF OUR HIDDEN ROAD-SIDE CAMERAS SHOWS YOUR CAR SPEEDING, SIR.

I SEE, OFFICER...

AND WHAT IF I WERE TO DISPUTE THAT THIS WAS MY CAR?

POINTLESS, SIR, THE REGISTRATION NUMBER IS CLEARLY VISIBLE.

AND IF I WERE TO CHALLENGE YOU ON EXACTLY WHEN THE PHOTO WAS TAKEN?

AS YOU SEE, SIR, THE CAMERA AUTOMATICALLY PRINTS THE DATE AND PRECISE TIME ON THE PHOTOGRAPH ITSELF...

AH YES... 00:06. 01:08:93...

I THINK THAT'S IRREFUTABLE PROOF, SIR.

YES...

...THAT I WAS AMONG THE FIRST TO HAVE AN L-REGISTRATION VEHICLE. OKAY, HOW MUCH DO YOU WANT FOR IT?

I'VE TOLD YOU, SIR, OFFENDERS ARE NOT PERMITTED TO PURCHASE THE ORIGINAL...

Alex PEATTIE + TAYLOR

WHAT ON EARTH DO YOU THINK YOU'RE DOING, CLIVE?

I'M JUST MUGGING UP ON THE L.B.W. LAW...

AFTER ALL, WE'LL HAVE TO TAKE TURNS UMPIRING WHEN OUR SIDE IS BATTING.

CLIVE, THIS IS YOUR THIRD TOUR WITH US. ARE YOU REALLY STILL IGNORANT OF THE MOST BASIC PRINCIPLES OF CRICKET?

BUT, ALEX, L.B.W.S ARE NOTORIOUSLY CONTENTIOUS DECISIONS AS THEY RELY TOTALLY ON THE UMPIRE'S JUDGEMENT AS TO THE BOUNCE, HEIGHT AND DIRECTION OF THE BALL...

EXACTLY, CLIVE. LOOK, I THINK I CAN SUM IT UP SIMPLY FOR YOU...

NO BATSMAN ON OUR TEAM IS EVER OUT L.B.W. WHILE ONE OF US IS UMPIRING, UNDERSTOOD?

ER... RIGHT...

1994

SOUTH AFRICA AND THE LABOUR PARTY WERE SUCCESSFULLY REBRANDED. THE I.R.A. TEMPORARILY CEASED TRADING. BONUSES AND PORSCHES WERE BACK AND GAVE RISE TO ROAD RAGE. THE CITY'S MONEY-MAKING METHODS WERE SUCCESSFULLY REPLICATED IN THE NATIONAL LOTTERY.

1995

PROUD BRITISH INSTITUTIONS WERE HUMBLED: WARBURGS FELL TO THE SWISS, AT BARINGS NICK LEESON BLEW HIS CHANCE OF A BONUS (AND EVERYONE ELSE'S) AND THE DEPUTY GOVERNOR OF THE BANK OF ENGLAND GAVE A NEW MEANING TO BOARDROOM EXCESSES, TO THE RELIEF OF THE FATCATS AT THE PRIVATISED UTILITY COMPANIES.

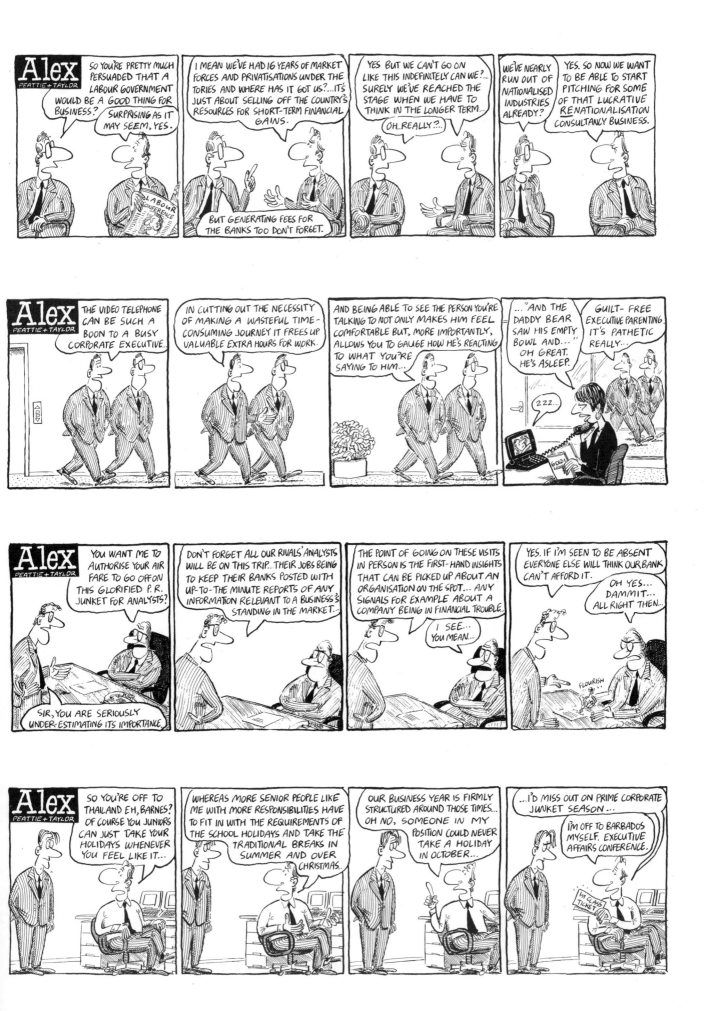

1996

THE BRITISH BEEF EXPORT INDUSTRY WAS TRIMMED TO THE BONE. THE CASE AGAINST THE MAXWELL BROTHERS SANK WITHOUT TRACE AND THE I.R.A. UNFASHIONABLY RELOCATED ITS CENTRE OF OPERATIONS TO DOCKLANDS. EURO '96 ADDED FURTHER TO THE CITY'S GRUELLING SUMMER HOSPITALITY BURDEN.

Alex PEATTIE + TAYLOR

YOU KNOW, COMPUTER GRAPHICS TECHNOLOGY IS SO ADVANCED THESE DAYS THAT PHOTOS CAN BE UNDETECTABLY DOCTORED TO ADD, REMOVE OR CHANGE PEOPLE WHO APPEAR IN THEM...

THERE ARE ACTUALLY COMMERCIALLY AVAILABLE SERVICES WHICH CAN, FOR EXAMPLE, TOUCH UP YOUR WEDDING PHOTO TO SEAMLESSLY INSERT A MISSING LOVED-ONE...

JUST IMAGINE HOW USEFUL THAT COULD BE WHEN ONE HAS A FORMAL PHOTOGRAPHIC RECORD OF A SOCIAL EVENT WHERE A GROUP OF FRIENDS IS GATHERED YET ONE PERSON IS UNAVOIDABLY ABSENT DUE TO CIRCUMSTANCES BEYOND HIS CONTROL...

SUCH AS HIS WIMPISHLY-LOW LEVEL OF ALCOHOL TOLERANCE?

I'D JUST LIKE TO BE IN A MAY BALL SURVIVORS' PHOTO FOR ONCE...

MAY BALL 1983
SURVIVORS' PHOTO

Alex PEATTIE + TAYLOR

WELL WITH EUROPEAN CUP FOOTBALL MATCHES ALL OVER ENGLAND THIS SUMMER, DO YOU THINK IT WILL IMPACT ON OUTLOOK AND MENTALITY HERE VIS-A-VIS EUROPE?

OH YES...

.. I THINK IT'LL STOP A LOT OF PEOPLE BEING SO INSULAR IN THEIR CULTURE, ONLY CONSIDERING THE BRITISH NATIONAL PERSPECTIVE... ESPECIALLY IN THE YOUNGER GENERATION...

I'M ALREADY HEARING A LOT OF THEM TALKING IN TERMS OF A WIDER CONTINENTAL HERITAGE AND OF AWARENESS OF THEIR DEEP-ROOTED EUROPEAN IDENTITY...

REALLY?   YES.

ONLY TO JUSTIFY THEIR ATTENDANCE OF UNPOPULAR LOW-PRESTIGE MATCHES BETWEEN 3RD RATE MINORITY COUNTRIES NONE OF US SENIORS BAGGED TICKETS TO...

BANK TICKET ALLOCATIONS

.. ER... I'VE ALWAYS SUPPORTED CROATIA ACTUALLY... IN FACT I'M SORT OF PART-CROATIAN...

Alex PEATTIE + TAYLOR

IT'S ONLY NATURAL FOR US TO BE CONCERNED ABOUT OUR HUSBANDS WORKING IN LONDON NOW THAT THE I.R.A. HAS RESUMED ITS TERRORIST CAMPAIGN.

YES INDEED.

IT'S SAD THAT AS A RESULT OF THE BREAKDOWN OF THE NORTHERN IRELAND PEACE TALKS THOSE SCUM HAVE TAKEN THE EXCUSE TO REVERT TO THEIR CYNICAL COWARDLY TACTICS OF THE PAST...

.. MOVING WITHOUT FEAR OF DETECTION IN LONDON AND RELISHING THE CONFUSION, DISRUPTION AND MISINFORMATION WHICH CAN ONLY FURTHER SERVE THEIR PURPOSE...

THEY REALLY ARE DESPICABLE...

SLAM

AH... HERE'S ONE OF THEM NOW...

SORRY I'M LATE, DARLING, ...ER... MY CAB WAS STOPPED AT A CHECKPOINT AND I MISSED MY TRAIN... AND THEN THEY CLOSED THE STATION DUE TO A SECURITY ALERT...

LYING RAT... JUST ADMIT YOU'VE BEEN OUT BOOZING...

SWAY

Alex PEATTIE + TAYLOR

APPARENTLY THAT WAS THE MOST AUTHENTIC AND NON-JUDGEMENTAL CONTEMPORARY PORTRAYAL OF YOUNG SCOTTISH INNER-CITY DRUG TAKERS EVER.

Trainspotting 18

IT'S NO EXCUSE, CLIVE.

PERSONALLY I THINK THE FILM-MAKERS WERE TOTALLY IRRESPONSIBLE. THEY SHOULD DEFINITELY HAVE DONE MORE TO ACTIVELY CONDEMN WHAT THOSE KIDS SLIP INTO...

AFTER ALL WE'RE TALKING ABOUT SOMETHING THAT CAN ALL TOO EASILY GET COMPLETELY OUT OF CONTROL.

YOU MEAN ADDICTION?

YES...

I MEAN, THE DICTION UP THERE IS BAD ENOUGH AS IT IS WITHOUT PEOPLE SLURRING THEIR SPEECH... I COULDN'T UNDERSTAND A BLITHERING WORD THEY SAID...

WHAT DO THEY TEACH THEM AT RADA?

1997

UNDER A NEW CORPORATE IDENTITY LABOUR FINALLY WON THE FRANCHISE TO RUN GREAT BRITAIN, BUT WERE SOON REVEALED AS CORPORATE RAIDERS AS THEY IMMEDIATELY SET ABOUT BREAKING IT UP. CHINA REACQUIRED A FORMER SUBSIDIARY IN AN AGREED BID. NICOLA HORLICK ENGAGED IN A FAMOUS GROUSE.

1998

THE REMAINING BITS OF THE UNITED KINGDOM WERE REPACKAGED AS "COOL BRITANNIA" IN PREPARATION FOR A RUMOURED SALE TO EUROPE. IN LONDON BRITISH BANKS MERGED WITH FOREIGN COMPETITORS BUT OUR CURRENCY DIDN'T. AT THE OSCARS THE BRITISH FILM INDUSTRY WAS SUNK BY THE TITANIC...